For my family, with whom
I am grateful to celebrate
–A. R.

For Mike, Tien, and Reid, always

–J. J. T.

BEACH LANE BOOKS
An imprint of Simon & Schuster Children's Publishing Division
1230 Avenue of the Americas, New York, New York 10020
Text © 2022 by Aimee Reid
Illustration © 2022 by Jing Jing Tsong
Book design by Rebecca Syracuse © 2022 by Simon & Schuster, Inc.
BEACH LANE BOOKS and colophon are trademarks of Simon & Schuster, Inc.
For information about special discounts for bulk purchases, please contact
Simon & Schuster Special Sales at 1-866-506-1949 or business@simonandschuster.com.
The Simon & Schuster Speakers Bureau can bring authors to your live event. For more
information or to book an event, contact the Simon & Schuster Speakers Bureau
at 1-866-248-3049 or visit our website at www.simonspeakers.com.
The text for this book was set in Haboro.
The illustrations for this book were rendered digitally.
Manufactured in China
0122 SCP
First Edition
10 9 8 7 6 5 4 3 2 1
Library of Congress Cataloging-in-Publication Data
Names: Reid, Aimee, author. | Tsong, Jing Jing, illustrator.
Title: First morning sun : a book of firsts / Aimee Reid ; illustrated by Jing Jing Tsong.
Description: First edition. | New York : Beach Lane Books, [2022] | Audience: Ages 0-8. | Audience: Grades K-1. |
Summary: With many firsts to experience and lots to see, a little one's life is full of wonder and discovery.
Identifiers: LCCN 2021003780 (print) | LCCN 2021003781 (ebook) | ISBN 9781534438842 (hardcover) | ISBN 9781534438859 (ebook)
Subjects: CYAC: Stories in rhyme. | Babies–Fiction. | Family life–Fiction. | Growth–Fiction. | LCGFT: Picture books.
Classification: LCC PZ8.3.R2663 Fi 2022 (print) | LCC PZ8.3.R2663 (ebook) | DDC [E]–dc23
LC record available at https://lccn.loc.gov/2021003780
LC ebook record available at https://lccn.loc.gov/2021003781

Aimee Reid

Jing Jing Tsong

First Morning Sun

A Book
of Firsts

Beach Lane Books · New York London Toronto Sydney New Delhi

First morning sun.
First day begun.

First tiny cry.
First lullaby.

First Grandma's rock.
First round-the-clock.

First special toy.
First laugh of joy.

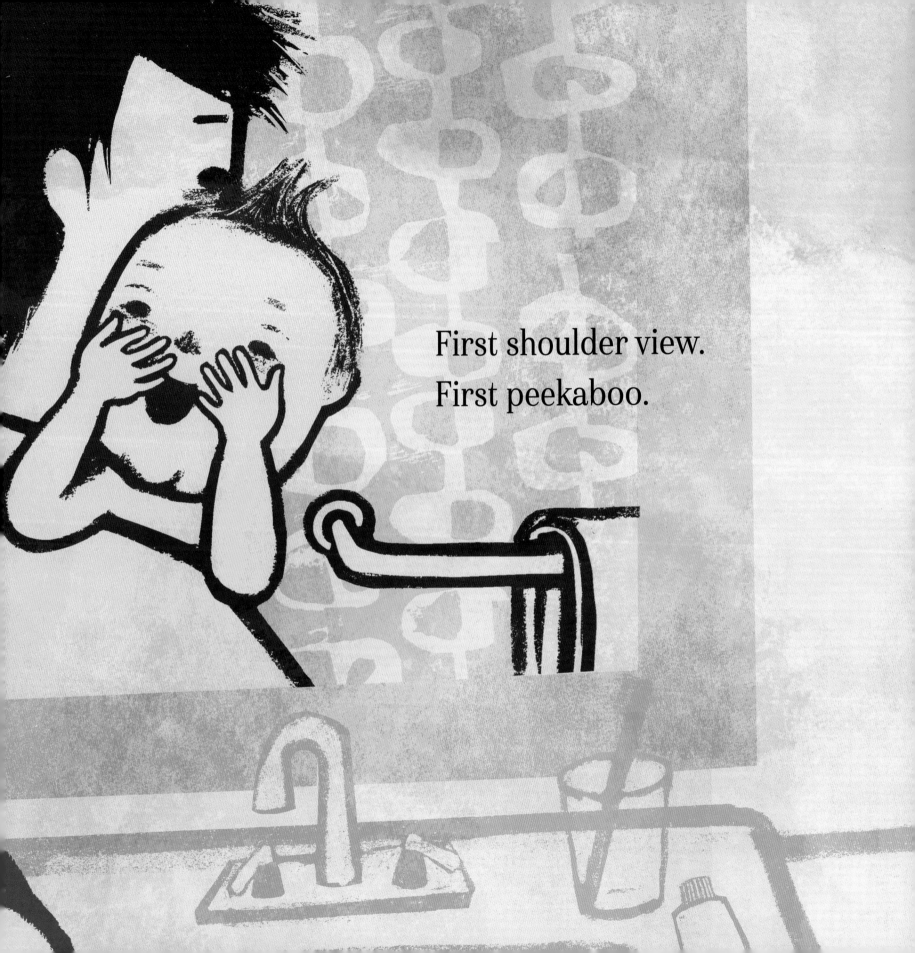

First shoulder view.
First peekaboo.

First baby talk.

First shaky walk.

First birthday treat.

First cake to eat.

First play pretend.
First real-life friend.

First Granddad's spin.

First ice cream grin.

First rolling wave.
First feeling brave.

First seek-and-hide.

First playground slide.

First work of art.

First feeling smart.

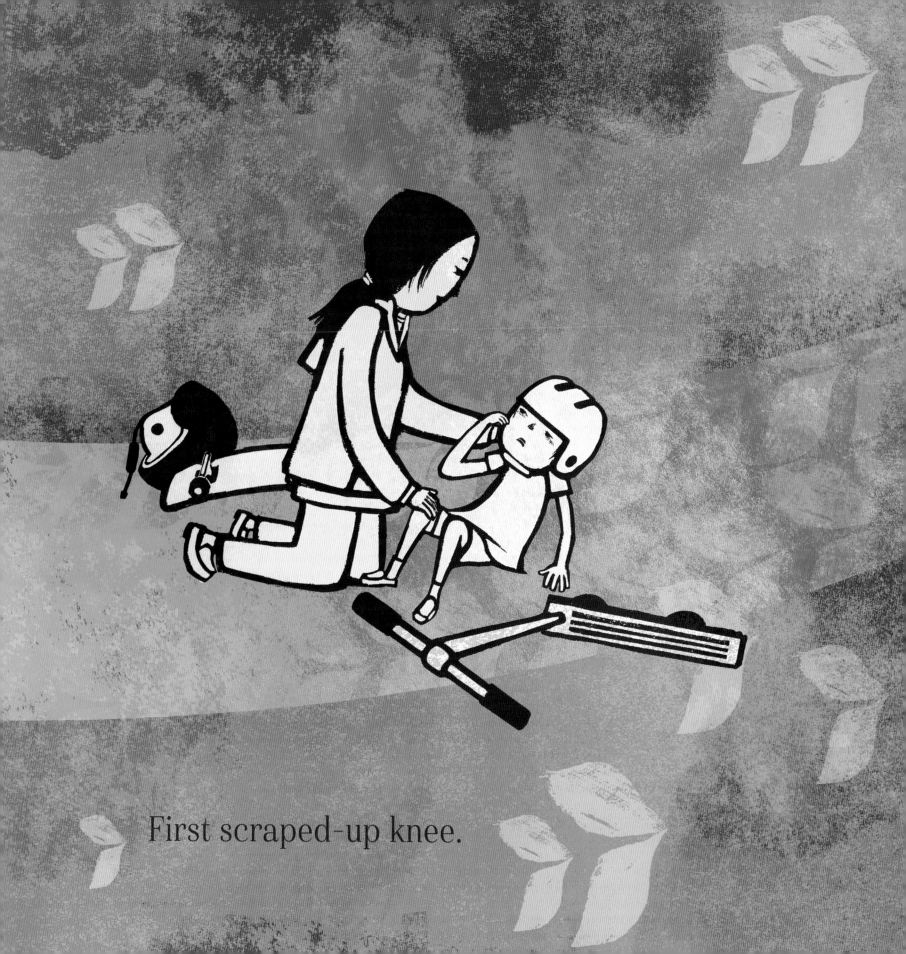

First scraped-up knee.

First climbing tree.

First school-door pause.

First crowd applause.

First holding tight.
First taking flight.

First sibling new.
More firsts for two.